A to Z Idioms

© Written and Illustrated by Jill Hahn.

AuthorHouse™
1663 Liberty Drive
Bloomington, IN 47403
www.authorhouse.com
Phone: 1-800-839-8640

Published by AuthorHouse 02/08/2012

ISBN: 978-1-4685-5254-6 (sc)

Library of Congress Control Number: 2012902352

authorHOUSE®

Thank you for supporting
my book !! ☺
Best wishes,

Jill Hahn

My book is dedicated to my Mom for teaching me the ABCs.

Special thanks to Kim Macfie and the outstanding staff
@ McKeown Elementary School
for their ongoing enthusiastic support.

Thanks to my students for their advice.

Thank you to my family and friends for encouraging me
to follow my dream of writing & illustrating a book. I love you!

Best wishes to teachers everywhere!

Jill Hahn is a fourth grade teacher who has always dreamed of publishing a book for kids. <u>A to Z Idioms</u> is her first book written & illustrated for children of all ages, a true *labor of love*.

<u>A to Z Idioms</u> was created by using handmade collage illustrations. Finishing this book has left her feeling *over the moon*.

Jill is bubbly, outgoing and is usually seen laughing. She enjoys music, jamming on her ukulele, mountain biking, playing ball, and being outdoors. She loves spending time with her awesome family & friends.

As the crow flies she lives near the Appalachian Trail in beautiful northern New Jersey with her hound dogs, Jack & Meadow. They can be found *snug as two bugs in a rug* on her studio couch while she works.

a Piece of Cake

Meaning: If something is a piece of cake, it is really easy.

The ants thought raiding the picnic was a piece of cake.
This was their lucky day thanks to a big break.
They were taking their goods back to the hill,
excited that they had accomplished their drill.

Right, Left, Right, Left

Butterflies in Your Stomach

Meaning: The nervous feeling before something important or stressful is known as butterflies in your stomach.

Rabbit was so nervous about his first race,
that he felt butterflies in his stomach's place.
He had trained for this moment for most of his life,
now he felt worry and strife.

ON YOUR MARK... GET SET!

Crocodile Tears

Meaning: If someone cries crocodile tears, they pretend to be upset or affected by something.

Young crocodile was scolded by her father
because earlier that day she was rude to her teacher, a real bother.
Although she didn't feel too terribly guilty,
she put on an act and cried two fake tears that were salty and silty.

SNIFF! SNIFF!

Down-to-Earth

Meaning: Someone who is down-to-earth is practical and realistic. It can also be used for things like ideas.

It was easy for him to get caught up in all the hype,
being an alien on a humans only planet type.
He knew he was special and quite unique, but he didn't let it go to his head.
He remained humble and down-to-earth instead.

Greetings Earthlings!

Early Bird Catches the Worm

Meaning: The early bird catches the worm means that if you start something early, you stand a better chance of success.

Mr. Robin groaned when his alarm rang at 5:30.
He knew, however, that catching the worm was easier bright and early.
So he didn't delay, but got up and started his day.
Much to the worm's dismay!

EEK! SHREIK!

Fish Out of Water

Meaning: If you are placed in a situation that is completely new and uncomfortable, you are like a fish out of water.

He felt like a fish out of water no doubt,
when he tried to swim with a school of piranhas instead of trout.
He was hoping for a friendly smile,
to assure him that he could hang for a while.

Ugh! Gulp!

GET YOUR GOAT

Meaning: If something gets your goat, it annoys you.

"We don't mean to get your goat,
but we love your stinky, furry coat!
We're not trying to be pesky or mean,
we would go away if you were clean."

BUZZ! BUZZ!

Hang Out to Dry

Meaning: If you hang someone out to dry, you abandon them when they are in trouble.

Chameleon should not have accepted his friends dare
to climb the laundry line with underwear.
From the ground he heard them laugh and yell, "Goodbye!"
as they let him hang out to dry.

Hey! Guys! Wait!

If You Are Given Lemons, Make Lemonade

Meaning: Always try to make the best of a bad situation.

"Look on the bright side," he replied
as the lemons around him sighed.
"Being made into juice might be nice,
at least we're not doomed to be Italian Ice."

Squish, Squash, Squeeze!

JUMP SHIP

Meaning: If you jump ship you leave a job or activity suddenly before it is finished.

The crabs decided to jump ship quickly,
the idea of ending up at the market made them feel sickly.
Eager to get back to the ocean floor for goodness sakes,
in fear of being made into crab cakes.

BLUB, BLUB

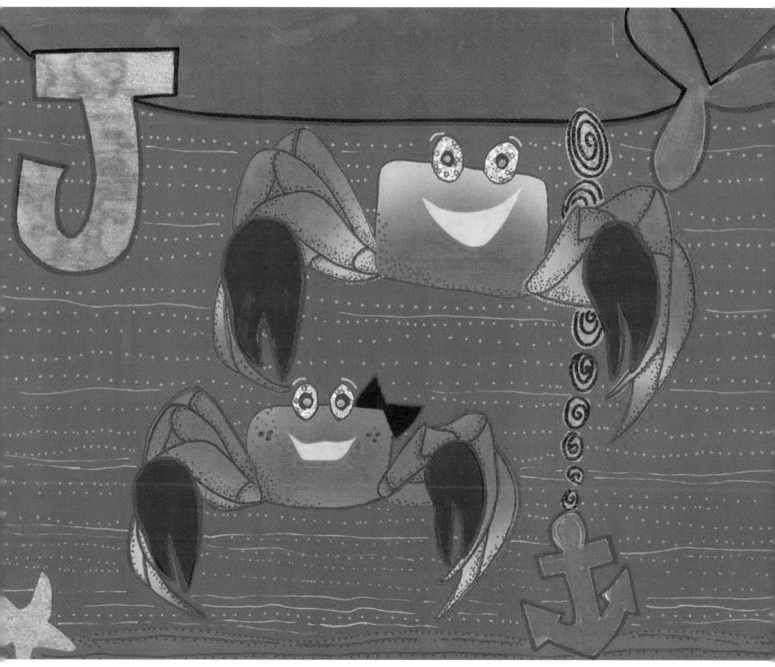

Knock on Wood

Meaning: This idiom is used to wish for good luck.

Hmmm, the woodpecker pondered about his hungry tummy.
I've wished on a shooting star and a lucky penny,
I even gave the magic genie lamp a rub.
I suppose I'll knock on wood in hopes of finding some grub.

Peck, Peck, Peck

Lend Me Your Ear

Meaning: If you lend an ear, you listen to what someone has to say.

Look here young elephant, lend me your ear.
The sight of a mouse is supposed to make you feel fear.
It seems silly, being as you're so huge and I am small.
But it's a fact. Thanks for the chat. That's all.

Pssst! Pssst!

Make a Mountain Out of a Molehill

Meaning: If somebody makes a mountain out of a molehill,
they exaggerate the importance or seriousness of a problem.

There's no reason to make a mountain out of a molehill, Sir.
We simply snuck this food without creating a stir.
True, we shouldn't be eating this at midnight.
Still it's not that serious of a problem, everything is alright.

Right, Left, Right, Left

 Night Owl

Meaning: A night owl is someone who goes to bed very late.

Once upon a time there lived a night owl
who would sit on his perch and scowl.
He wanted to sleep during the night and not day,
but he was nocturnal so he had no say.

 Hoot! Hoot!

ON THE TIP OF MY TONGUE

Meaning: If a word is on the tip of your tongue, you know the word, but you just can't quite remember it at the moment.

Our mother warned us about the threat of a slithering stranger.
We know better than to put ourselves in danger.
"Unless you can tell us the secret password," they sung.
Ssso Sssorry, I can't remember, but it's on the tip of my tongue.

HISSSSSS

Pain in the Neck

Meaning: If something is very annoying and always disturbing you, it is a pain in the neck.

My house is so heavy and really slows me down.
On the plus side I can travel freely from town to town.
It can be a real pain in the neck lugging my shell around,
Although it is nice having a place to sleep safe and sound.

Zzzz Zzzz

Meaning: The queen bee is a woman who holds the most important position in a place.

Being the Queen Bee is a big responsibility.
You need strength, courage, and common sensibility.
I'm in charge of the workers and drones of the hive.
I laid 2,000 eggs yesterday and now I have to keep the larvae alive.

Rack Your Brain

Meaning: If you rack your brain, you think very hard when trying to remember something.

Remind me again, what do cats eat?
Umm... cat food and mice and meat.
You'll need to rack your brain and think about why,
that feline might be giving us the hungry eye!

Meow

SKATE ON THIN ICE

Meaning: If someone is skating on thin ice, they are taking a big risk.

The penguins partied for a long time.
They danced and sang, feeling sublime.
The occasion had been a roll of the dice,
knowing they were skating on thin ice.

CREAK, CRACK

True Colors

Meaning: If someone shows their true colors, they show themselves as they really are.

Peacock was never much of an attention seeker.
He was quiet and shy and meager.
Then one day a friend bet him five dollars,
to be brave and show off his true colors.

Oooooh Aaaaah

Up in the Air

Meaning: If a matter is up in air, no decision has been made and there is uncertainty about it.

My plans are up in the air, thinking about what I should do today.
Perhaps I'll do the same thing as yesterday!
Flying squirrels are meant to have fun,
soaring freely from tree to tree in the shade and the sun.

Whooosh!

Vicious Cycle

Meaning: A vicious cycle is a sequence of events that make each other worse.

Building and rebuilding can be such a vicious cycle.
People swat at my web and I have to recycle.
Sometimes they walk through it and shout,
spending the next six minutes freaking out!

Thwapp!

WHEN PiGS FLY

Meaning: When pigs fly is an expression used if something is unlikely to happen or even impossible.

Pig wanted to be able to take flight,
like a butterfly or bird or a rocket out of sight.
The other farm animals boomed, "No way! When pigs fly!"
He was determined to keep giving it a try.

OiNK! OiNK!

X-MARKS THE SPOT

Meaning: This is used to say where something is located or hidden.

The pirates' treasure map had been misplaced,
dropped overboard in their hurry and haste.
Octopus found the soggy map with a red x-marks the spot,
so excited that he shot off an inkblot when he realized that he had hit the jackpot.

AARGH!

You Can't Teach an Old Dog New Tricks

Meaning: It is difficult to make someone change the way they do something when they have been doing it the same way for a long time.

Jackson and Meadow are seven-years old.
They are stubborn and lazy and bold.
They only like basking in the sun and gnawing on sticks.
You know what they say; you can't teach an old dog new tricks.

Bow Wow

Zip It

Meaning: This is used to tell someone to be quiet.

I think her mane is creative and original.
On the contrary, I think it's funny and hysterical.
Zebra overheard the birds' gossip behind her back.
Wishing they would zip it and cut her some slack.

Shhh!

CPSIA information can be obtained
at www.ICGtesting.com
Printed in the USA
273303LV00001B